INTO THE WILD

Yet another misadventure

Also by Doreen Cronin

Bloom

Bounce

The Chicken Squad #1: *The First Misadventure*
The Chicken Squad #2: *The Case of the Weird*
Blue Chicken: The Next Misadventure

Click, Clack, Boo!
Click, Clack, Ho! Ho! Ho!
Click, Clack, Moo: Cows That Type
Click, Clack, Peep!
Click, Clack, Quackity-Quack
Click, Clack, Splish, Splash
Dooby Dooby Moo
Duck for President
Giggle, Giggle, Quack
M.O.M. (Mom Operating Manual)
Stretch
Thump, Quack, Moo
Wiggle

THE CHICKEN SQUAD

INTO THE WILD

Yet another misadventure

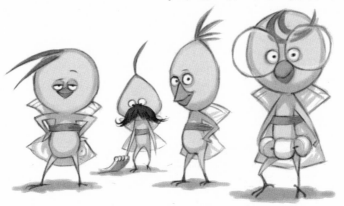

Doreen Cronin

Illustrated by Stephen Gilpin

Cover by Kevin Cornell

A Caitlyn Dlouhy Book

Atheneum Books for Young Readers

atheneum   New York   London   Toronto   Sydney   New Delhi

atheneum

ATHENEUM BOOKS FOR YOUNG READERS
An imprint of Simon & Schuster Children's Publishing Division
1230 Avenue of the Americas, New York, New York 10020

For information about special discounts for bulk purchases, please contact Simon & Schuster Special Sales at 1-866-506-1949 or business@simonandschuster.com.
The Simon & Schuster Speakers Bureau can bring authors to your live event. For more information or to book an event, contact the Simon & Schuster Speakers Bureau at 1-866-248-3049 or visit our website at www.simonspeakers.com.
Book design by Sonia Chaghatzbanian
The text for this book was set in Garth Graphic.
The illustrations for this book were rendered digitally.
Manufactured in the United States of America
0316 FFG
First Edition
10 9 8 7 6 5 4 3 2 1
CIP data for this book is available from the Library of Congress.
ISBN 978-1-4814-5046-1
ISBN 978-1-4814-5048-5 (eBook)

For the McCarthy clan, with love

—D. C.

For Kevin. Sincere thanks
for all the help on this.

—S. G.

INTO THE WILD

Yet another misadventure

Introductions

Welcome to the yard!

The name is John Joseph Tully; J. J. for short. I was a search-and-rescue dog for seven years, but my days of dangerous missions and daring rescues are behind me. Sure, I miss being a hero, but Barbara's backyard is an okay kind of place once you get used to it. Everybody knows the rules—and everybody follows 'em. Except for the

chickens, and the neighbor who likes to run his power saw a little too early in the morning. Luckily, somebody keeps chewing through his extension cord— but I don't know anything about that.

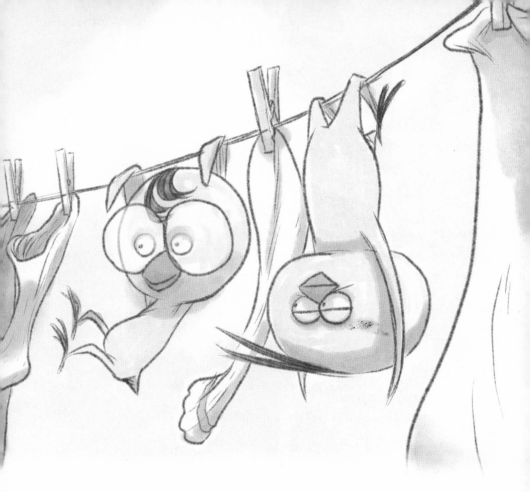

As for the chickens, I found them on the clothesline this morning, blowing in the wind between the socks and the pillowcases. Here they are:

Dirt: Short, yellow, fuzzy

Real Name: Peep

Specialty: Foreign languages, math,
colors, computer codes

Sugar: Short, yellow, fuzzy

Real Name: Little Boo

Specialty: Breaking and entering, interrupting

Poppy: Short, yellow, fuzzy

Real Name: Poppy

Specialty: Watching the shoe
(will explain later)

Sweetie: Short, yellow, fuzzy

Real Name: Sweet Coconut Louise

Specialty: None that I can see

"How did you get up there?" I asked them.

"Wouldn't you love to know?" replied Sugar.

"How long do you plan on staying up there?" I asked.

"Until we have to pee," said Sweetie.

"Wait, were we supposed to get down to pee?" asked Poppy.

Well, that's about all the chicken

I can take in one day. They got themselves up there; they'll get themselves down. They're all yours. I have an extension cord to chew (but you didn't hear it from me . . .).

Chapter 1

I got a bad feeling about that new box over there," said Sugar. She pointed to a strange wooden structure on the other side of the yard. It stood on tall legs a few feet off the ground.

"Why?" asked Dirt.

"Why would Barbara sneak a weird box into our yard under the cover of night? What doesn't she want us to know? What is she hiding?"

"Actually," said Dirt, "Barbara's been out there hammering and sawing and building every single afternoon for the last two weeks."

"I think I would have noticed that, Dirt," said Sugar. She hopped up onto

the picnic bench. "I'm very observant."

"She also dismantled our chicken coop yesterday and moved it to the other side of the yard."

"I think I would have noticed that, Dirt," said Sugar.

"You may have been napping," suggested Dirt.

"What I hear you saying," said Sugar, "is that Barbara built a top-secret box and then top secretly moved our chicken coop far, far away from it. That's what I hear you saying. . . . "

"I didn't say that . . . ," said Dirt.

"Fine," answered Sugar, "but that's what I heard."

"Okay, well, why don't we just go take a closer look? There's a ramp that leads right up to the front of the box," suggested Dirt. "Maybe we can get some more information."

"We have no idea what kind of wild creature is in there!" said Sugar. "All we know for sure is that whatever it is, it is very, very dangerous."

"How do we know that?" asked Dirt.

"If it wasn't wild and dangerous, why would Barb keep it in a box? Only wild, dangerous animals are KEPT IN BOXES!"

"But we live in a box," said Dirt, "and we're not dangerous."

"Speak for yourself," replied Sugar.

"Anyway," said Dirt, "I think what we need to do here is observe and investigate."

"What I hear you saying," said Sugar, "is that this is an extremely dangerous

situation, lives are at stake, and we should proceed with caution. That's what I hear you saying. . . ."

"I didn't say that," said Dirt. "I didn't say that at all."

"Fine," said Sugar. "But that's what I heard."

Chapter 2

"Here are the facts," announced Sugar. She pointed to the diagram on the chicken-coop wall.

"Barbara was attacked by a wild animal and barely managed to escape. She somehow captured the dangerous beast and has secured it in a top-secret maximum-security box.

We are all in imminent danger."

"Those are not facts," said Dirt. "A fact is something you know for sure. All of what you just said is pure speculation."

"Listen, pal," said Sugar. "You don't

know what I know, and I don't know what you know. Agreed?"

"These are the *actual* facts," continued Dirt. She said them out loud as she listed them on the wall:

1. There is a new box in the yard.

2. Barbara built it herself out of wood and wire.

3. It has a latch on it.

4. We don't know what's in it.

"Why don't we just go look?" suggested Sweetie.

"Oh, kid," sighed Sugar. "You can't just walk up to a top-secret maximum-security box and peek in it! Something might jump out of it! You have to *watch* the creature—get a *feel* for how it lives and what it's thinking."

"You mean spy on it?" asked Sweetie.

"Of course not!" said Sugar. "I mean hide ourselves at a safe distance and watch everything it does while making sure it never sees us. The technical term is *surveillance*, otherwise known as a 'stakeout.' A dangerous mission, for sure, but—"

"Sounds like spying," interrupted Sweetie.

"I prefer *observing*," said Dirt.

"AS I was saying," continued Sugar, "surveillance is dangerous work. You'll be tired; you'll be hungry; and you'll see things a chicken should never see." She turned to her sister.

"Dirt, walk us through. . . ."

Dirt stepped up to the wall. "Sugar and I," she began, "will be up here in the maple tree. It will give us good cover, and we'll have a clear view of the box."

"Got it," said Sugar.

"Sweetie, you're next. You'll be observing from the gutter that runs along the back edge of the house. It's a different angle, so you might be able to see things that we can't see."

"Got it," said Sweetie.

"Poppy," said Sugar. "You stay with the shoe. If the creature spots us, it might get angry and agitated. If I whistle, you

run and get Mom or J. J. for backup. Got it?"

"Got it," said Poppy.

"But if I hoot like an owl," explained Sugar, "that just means I'm hungry and you should bring me more marsh-mallows."

"Got it," said Poppy. "Wait, you have marshmallows?"

"Stick with me here! But if you hear a *honking* sound," added Sugar. "That means I'm chilly and you should bring me a sweater."

"Got it," said Poppy.

"But if I make a *quacking* sound like a duck—" started Sugar.

"Let's move on," interrupted Dirt.

"What I hear you saying," said Sugar, "is that I've given Poppy too many noises to keep track of and I should probably keep things simple. Not to mention, owls are nocturnal and do not hoot during the day. . . ."

"That's actually exactly what I meant," said Dirt, surprised.

"Say what you mean, kid," said

Sugar. "SAY WHAT YOU MEAN."

Sugar pulled four baggies out of a box and gave one to each chicken.

"I've taken the liberty of putting together spy kits for each of you. Inside it you'll find an observation log, binoculars, marshmallows, and a fake mustache."

"I thought you said we weren't spying!" said Sweetie.

"Pipe down, kid," whispered Sugar. "I don't know how to spell 'surveillance.'"

"Now let's head out," said Sugar. "Keep your eyes open, write everything down, and we'll meet back here in three minutes."

"Do you think three minutes is enough time to observe and gather information, Sugar? Or—" asked Dirt.

"This is SERIOUS BUSINESS, kid," interrupted Sugar. She turned around wearing her fake mustache and a belt made out of marshmallows. "Your obsession with details is going to undermine all our observations!"

Dirt opened her beak to say something, but she changed her mind.

Chapter 3

What is it?" asked Sugar, sitting behind her sister. "A polar bear? A lion? A shark?" Dirt and Sugar had a clear view from a tree limb about fifteen feet above the ground.

"The box is in the shade, and whatever is inside the box, it's kind of grayish, so I can't make it out. But

I don't think it's big enough to be a polar bear or a lion. And, well . . . I'm pretty sure we can rule out a shark in a box."

"Sharks can be gray," said Sugar. "And we haven't *observed* long enough to rule anything out just yet. KEEP AN OPEN MIND!"

"I'm ruling out shark," said Dirt.

"Suit yourself. What is the not-a-shark *doing*?" asked Sugar impatiently.

"I can see a flash of white and what I think is a food bowl. I think it's chewing," said Dirt, her binoculars trained on the box.

"Write that down," said Sugar. Dirt lowered her binoculars and picked up the observation log.

A few seconds went by.

"What's it doing now?" asked Sugar.

Dirt picked her binoculars back up. "Chewing," she said.

"Write that down," said Sugar. Dirt lowered her binoculars and picked up the observation log.

A few seconds went by.

"What's it doing now?" asked Sugar.

Dirt picked her binoculars back up. "Chewing," she repeated.

"Write that down," said Sugar. "Sharks chew. Are you sure it's not a shark?"

"Wouldn't it be easier if I just tell you what I see and *you* write it down in the log?" said Dirt.

"No one said surveillance was easy, kid," answered Sugar. "If I do all the work, how will you learn anything?"

Dirt shook her head and turned her attention back to the binoculars.

"It stopped chewing," announced Dirt.

"Write that down," said Sugar. "Every detail is important."

Sugar and Dirt sat in silence for a minute. Then Sugar took out her own binoculars and focused on the box.

"Time to call it a day, kid. Three minutes is up."

"I'm still not sure three minutes is enough time to really observe something and gather information," said Dirt.

Sugar turned around, her mouth full of marshmallows. "Forget the time!"

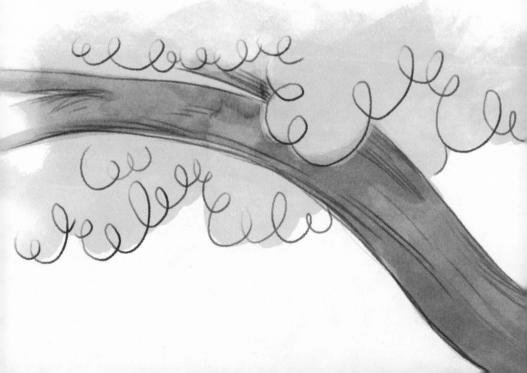

she mumbled. "Let me see the log." She
read Dirt's entries out loud:

Watching the creature,
Chewing, chewing, chewing,
  stop.
I like carrots, too.
Watching the creature,

Hopping, hopping, hopping,
stop.
Are you dangerous?

"I bring you to your first stakeout and you spend all your time writing poetry?" Sugar slammed the observation log closed.

"It was an accident," said Dirt.

"Poetry is never an accident, kid," replied Sugar.

Dirt opened her beak to say something, and then she changed her mind.

"I don't want to embarrass you in front of the squad," said Sugar, lowering her voice, "but I didn't see the hopping you claim to have seen in your log. You might want to take that part out before we report back to headquarters."

"You may have been napping," said Dirt.

"Happens on surveillance all the time, kid." Sugar chuckled. "Especially the long ones."

Dirt stared at Sugar for a moment and then packed up her binoculars and observation log. She waited until her sister was out of earshot.

"Three minutes," she muttered to herself. "Three minutes!"

Chapter 4

Listen up, squad!" said Sugar. "The bad news is we still have no idea what's in the box. The other bad news is Dirt used all her surveillance time to write poetry."

"I didn't do it on purpose!" protested Dirt.

Sugar rolled her eyes. "So unless

Sweetie observed something we didn't, I'm pretty sure we will never get close enough to the box to find out what's in it, and we should proceed as if it is a dangerous, wild animal—possibly a shark—and we are all in imminent danger."

"We ruled out shark!" yelled Dirt.

"No, kid, YOU ruled out shark, and I'm not completely comfortable with that. . . ."

"Sweetie," sighed Dirt. "Can you read us what you have in your observation log?"

"No," replied Sweetie.

"Why not?" asked Dirt.

"Spying is wrong," said Sweetie. "I climbed up to the gutter, just like you said, but I felt funny watching someone without his or her permission. So I slid down the pipe, rolled across the lawn, and came back here."

"How did we miss that?" asked Dirt.

"Apparently, I wasn't the only one napping," replied Sugar.

"But, based on your observations," continued Sweetie, "it sounds to me like there is a rabbit in the box."

"Why in the world would you say that?" demanded Sugar.

"Dirt's poem about chewing and hopping," answered Sweetie. "That's what rabbits do."

"I told you it was poem," grumbled Sugar.

Dirt paced back and forth excitedly. "So your hypothesis based on our observations is that the creature in the box is a rabbit!"

"So what I hear you saying," remarked Sugar, "is that three minutes

of skillful observation was plenty of time to gather information, form a hypothesis, AND take a nap! That's what I hear you saying!"

"I think what I'm saying is that if it eats like a rabbit and hops like a rabbit, it's probably a rabbit," said Sweetie.

"You've come a long way, kid," said Sugar.

"Thanks, sis!" said Sweetie.

"All right, kid," said Sugar, "enough blubbering."

"Rabbits aren't dangerous, are they?" asked Poppy.

"Not at all," replied Sugar. "Unless you're a carrot."

"Then why is it in a box?" asked Poppy.

"Rabbits are helpless," explained Sugar. "They can only eat salad; they can't handle the stairs; and I'm pretty sure the ears are just for show."

"Uh-oh!" cried Dirt from the door. "We have a really big problem!"

"We sure do, kid," said Sugar. "I

think I just ruined Easter for Poppy."

"No! Look!" said Dirt. "Look at the rabbit box! The door is wide open, and the rabbit is gone!"

"Oh no! Poor bunny!" cried Sweetie. "It will never survive on its own!"

"We're going after it!" declared Sugar. "Grab the emergency-survival kits!"

"We don't have emergency-survival kits," announced Dirt.

"We have our spy kits!" suggested Poppy. "Will they help us in an emergency?"

"Fake mustaches, marshmallows, and observation logs?" said Sugar, deep in thought. "Perfect!!"

The chickens zipped up their plastic baggies and lined up at the door.

"C'mon, squad!!" yelled Sugar. "Into the wild!" She waited until they were a few feet away from the chicken coop. "Now put on your mustaches and marshmallow belts; it's for your own safety!"

Chapter 5

The wilderness is a lot farther away than I thought," said Sugar, breathing heavily. "We should camp out here and wait for the bad weather to pass." Sugar tapped her head. "Survival skills, kid."

"You're right. There is a line of dark clouds approaching," said Dirt.

"I meant the sun," Sugar pointed out. "It's really hot. In fact, according to the compass, it's going to be a real scorcher today. My instincts tell me it's probably going to be close to two hundred degrees. Let's set up a tarp for shade and wait it out."

"Compasses don't predict weather," explained Dirt.

"We need to hydrate," said Sugar, ignoring her. "Let's stop here and fill our canteens."

"That's J. J.'s dog bowl,"' said Dirt. "He really doesn't like it when we go in there. Plus, I'm pretty sure it has, you know, dog spit in it. That is not clean water."

"Clean water? Is that what you think you need to survive? The last thing you need to survive is clean water!!"

"Every living thing needs clean water," said Dirt. "It may actually be one of the most important things. . . ."

Sugar ignored her sister again. "Hand me the canteen!" she demanded.

"We don't have canteens," replied Dirt. "And the sky is actually getting pretty dark; I think we should keep moving and stay ahead of it."

"Come on, chickens," announced Sugar. "For once, Dirt is right. We have to keep moving! Head count! One!"

"Two!" yelled Dirt.

"Three!" yelled Poppy.

The chickens waited.

"Close enough!" announced Sugar. "Let's move!"

"Hang on, Sugar," said Dirt. "We have to stick together in the wilderness. I'll

find Sweetie!" She turned around and headed back across the yard.

Sugar and Poppy set up a pillow-case for shade and played hangman in their observation logs while they waited.

"Found her!" yelled Dirt a few minutes later, walking under the

pillowcase with Sweetie right behind
her. Dirt was wearing a headlamp. Her
arms were full and her backpack was
overflowing.

"What is all that junk?" demanded
Sugar.

"There's a storm coming. I foraged
for berries, gathered firewood, and

used the hose to fill the baggie with fresh water!"

"I see." Sugar stared at her sister for a minute, nodding her head up and down. "Did you bring my lavender eye pillow and the jelly beans?"

"Um, no," replied Dirt.

"You wouldn't last a day in the wild without me, kid. Not one day."

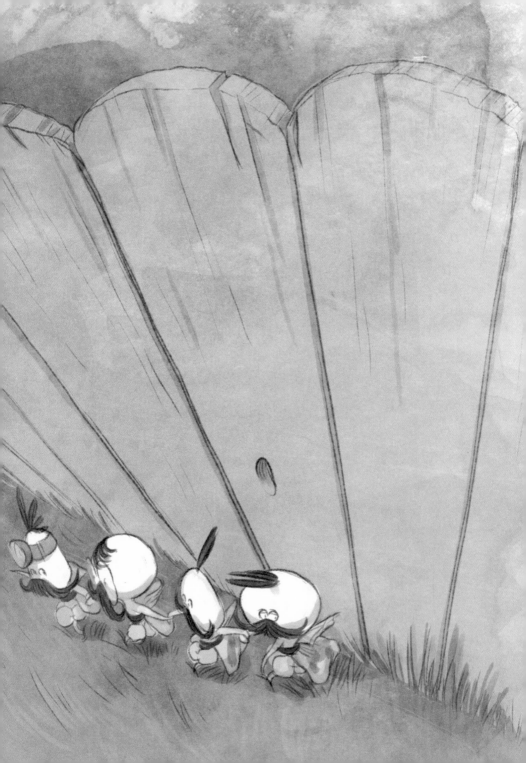

Chapter 6

Rabbits like to stay close to cover," said Dirt, leading the squad along the long back fence of the yard. "Try to think like a rabbit," she continued. "Which way would a rabbit go?"

"If I were a rabbit, I would go that way." Sugar pointed.

"If I were a rabbit," said Dirt, "I

wouldn't go that way because that's the way to the mall, and I would sense the vibrations of the heavy traffic."

"Exactly," said Sugar, turning around. "And when I sensed those vibrations, I would *turn around and go that way*, behind the tomato patch, and through the hole in fence that we dug last year to reach the trampoline in the neighbor's yard."

"If I were a rabbit," said Dirt, "my keen hearing would pick up on all those kids in the yard with the trampoline, and I would determine that it might not be the best way to go."

"I gotta hand it to you, kid," said Sugar.

"You're a better fake rabbit than I am."

"That means so much to me, Sugar," answered Dirt. "Thank you."

"All right, kid," said Sugar, turning serious. "Enough blubbering."

The sky grew dark, and the chickens pressed even closer to the fence for some cover from the wind.

"What are we going to do when we find the rabbit?" asked Sweetie.

"Throw the pillowcase over his head and drag him back to safety. That rabbit has no business in the wild," answered Sugar.

"The bag part sounds a little . . . extreme," said Dirt. Hard drops of rain bounced off their heads. "We can just gently lead him back to the yard."

"Do rabbits actually live in the wild?" asked Sweetie.

"Of course," replied Dirt. The chickens raised the tarp up over their heads for cover from the storm.

"How do they protect themselves without marshmallows and mustaches?" asked Sweetie.

"Excellent question," said Sugar.

"Mostly they run," answered Dirt. "They are also are very good at hiding and staying perfectly still."

"Speaking of still, doesn't the yard seem kind of quiet?" asked Sweetie.

"Yeah, where is everybody?" asked Poppy. "I don't hear any birds or see any squirrels. . . ."

"Good observation, Poppy," said Dirt. "Lots of animals have the instinct to take cover and lay low when they sense bad weather or danger."

"Maybe we should . . . do that too?" suggested Poppy. He looked up at the dark sky.

"Chickens don't run from danger, kid," said Sugar, rain dripping from the corners of her wet mustache. A deep boom of thunder opened up the sky and shook the fence. Lightning cracked right on its heels, and the rain came down so hard, it knocked the chickens to the ground.

"What should we do?" asked Sweetie, her eyes wide.

"RUN!!!!" yelled Sugar.

Chapter 7

It's too far to the chicken coop!" yelled Dirt, struggling to see in the pouring rain. "We'll make a run for the rabbit hutch! Keep one wing on the fence—it will guide us to the other side of the yard! STAY CLOSE!"

"The water is rising!" yelled Poppy, holding his wings up in the air to keep them dry. "Help!" A gust of wind lifted him off his feet and blew him ten feet back.

Dirt, Sugar, and Sweetie ran back to him, fighting their way through the torrential rain.

"Keep your wings down!!" Sugar yelled over the storm. "Otherwise, we'll blow all over the yard!"

"We need to tie ourselves together!" yelled Dirt. The wind blew her feathers straight back from her face.

"With what?" asked Poppy.

Dirt looked around frantically. "Our mustaches!"

"Good thinking!" yelled Sugar. The chickens ripped the mustaches off one at a time.

"Ouch!"

"Ouch!"

"Ouch!"

"Ouch!"

Then they tied themselves together and trudged through the rain and the mud, fighting through the wind every step of the way. A giant puddle at the bottom of the rabbit-hutch ramp blocked their way.

"Can we go through it?" yelled Sugar.

Dirt tossed a rock into the puddle and watched it disappear beneath the surface. "Too deep!"

"Head count!" yelled Dirt. "One!" The water rose up over their ankles.

"I'm one!" yelled Sugar. "I'm always one! Start over!" The water rose up to the tips of their wings.

"You can't always be one, Sugar! Head count starts with whoever who calls the head count! That's a rule of the wild!"

"Do chickens float?" yelled Poppy. The water was up to their necks.

"I think wild chickens can float!" said Sweetie. "Are we wild chickens?"

"Don't be ridiculous!" yelled Sugar. "We were born and raised in a heated box! We are not wild chickens!!"

"Head count!" Dirt and Sugar yelled at the same time.

"ONE!!" Dirt and Sugar called at the same time.

"I AM A WILD CHICKEN!" yelled Poppy. He dove into the water and floated on his back, a marshmallow under each wing, kicking his legs as fast as he could.

"Head count!" he called. "ONE!" His mustache pulled Sweetie in right behind him.

"TWO!" yelled Sweetie.

"THREE!" yelled Sugar, following Sweetie.

"FOUR!" yelled Dirt, following Sugar.

Exhausted, Poppy crawled up the

ramp, pulling on his mustache rope. One by one, the chickens pulled one another out of the water and then dragged one another to the top, diving into the rabbit hutch for cover.

A blast of wind blew the door shut behind them.

"I had no idea we could float!" said Sweetie.

"It was the marshmallow, kid," said Sugar, still out of breath. "The marshmallows are filled with air, so they float."

"So that's why you put them in the emergency survival kits!" said Sweetie.

"Exactly," said Sugar. She looked over at Dirt and shrugged.

"Head count," said Dirt, frazzled and out of breath. "One!"

"Two!"

"Three!"

"Four!"

"Five!"

"Five??" asked Sugar.

Chapter 8

Dirt, Sugar, Poppy, and Sweetie turned around to see the rabbit emerging from a dark corner of the hutch.

"We've been looking all over for you!" cried Dirt. "We thought you made a break for it and ran back into the wild!"

"You must be the chickens that were

spying on me from the maple tree and the gutter along the back of the house," said the rabbit.

"I told you it was spying!" said Sweetie.

"I prefer *observing*," added Dirt.

"You knew you were under surveillance?" asked Sugar. "But, how?"

"I'm a wild animal, kid," said the rabbit. "I've got instincts. I know when I'm being watched."

"Listen, Sparkles, we're the ones out in the wild with nothing but mustaches and marshmallows. You're the one in a bunny box, eating salad out of a bowl." Sugar grabbed a piece of the rabbit's lettuce and took a big chomp.

"My name is not Sparkles," said the rabbit.

"It is to me," replied Sugar.

"You can't do that. You can't just change somebody's name," answered the rabbit.

"There are no rules in the wild,

kid," replied Sugar. "Deal with it."

"What were you doing in that box?" asked Dirt.

"It's my hiding box," answered the rabbit. "Barbara built it into the hutch for me. Lots of rabbits have them. I sensed the storm and came in here."

"Sensed the storm?" said Sugar suspiciously. "What kind of bunny mumbo jumbo is that?"

"Like I said," replied the rabbit. "I'm a wild animal. I can sense things. . . ."

"Listen, kid," said Sugar, "if you want to pretend you're a wild animal with *special senses*, well, you know what, bunny, that's okay by me. Sometimes I pretend that I crashed to Earth on a meteorite and that's how I got my superpowers of survival and surveillance."

"I really am a wild animal," said the rabbit. "And I really do have heightened senses."

"You're a dreamer, kid," said Sugar. "I like that about you. Don't change."

"Your hiding box is just like my old

shoe!" said Poppy. "It helps me feel safe, and it doesn't smell very good."

"That's my litter box, kid," said the rabbit. "The hiding box is on the other side."

"Come look!" cried Sweetie. "The rain stopped, and it's beautiful!" The chickens and the rabbit rushed toward the door.

"Is it a rainbow?" asked Poppy.

"No, it's MOM!" yelled Sweetie. "She's coming up the ramp to save us!"

"Uh-oh," mumbled Sugar.

Moosh swung the door open and gathered up all her chicks.

"Did you sense that we were in danger, Mom?" asked Poppy.

"No," replied Moosh. "Sweetie left me a note and a pair of binoculars. I was watching you from the high perch in the chicken coop the whole time."

"You were *spying* on us?" demanded Sugar.

"I call it *observing*," said Moosh.

"Well, it sure feels like spying to me!" Sugar protested. She turned to face Sweetie. "Why would you leave Mom a note?"

"Just a survival skill I picked up," replied Sweetie.

"From who?" asked Sugar.

"From Mom," replied Sweetie.

"You worked very nicely together," said Moosh. "I loved what you did with the mustaches and the marshmallows, too," she added. "I'm so proud of all of you." She used her beak to cut through the mustache rope.

"Thanks, Mom," said Dirt. "I guess we're all still wild chickens at heart."

"I guess so," said Moosh. "By the way, you're all grounded for leaving the coop without telling me where you were going. Except for Sweetie, of course."

Sugar glared at her sister.

"Survival skills, kid," announced Sweetie.

Epilogue

It took a while, but Sparkles the bunny (the name kind of stuck), eventually felt safe enough to come out of the hutch and wander around a bit. Of course, I walked him around the yard a few times to help him get a feel for things.

As for the squad, Moosh decided that the best way to dry the chickens

out was to send them back up to the clothesline. They fluffed up real nice and even smelled like sunshine. Sparkles "observed" them and wrote a poem about it:

Blowing in the breeze
Poppy, Sweetie, Sugar, Dirt
Fluffy trouble birds

"I wouldn't stand under there if I were you . . . ," said Poppy.

"Is that rain?" asked Sparkles, looking up at Sweetie on the clothesline.

"Keep dreaming, kid," said Sugar. "Keep dreaming."

Doreen Cronin is the author of the Chicken Squad series as well as many bestselling books, including *Click, Clack, Ho! Ho! Ho!*; *Click, Clack, Peep!*; and the Caldecott Honor Book *Click, Clack, Moo: Cows That Type*. Her hobbies include lurking in the shadows and solving imaginary crimes. She lives in Brooklyn, New York. Visit her at DoreenCronin.com.

Stephen Gilpin lives and draws pictures for brilliant children in a cave just north of Hiawatha, Kansas, with his wife, Angie; their kids; and an infestation of dogs.